Has spring already arrived

Has spring already arrived

Trường Hà Vũ Toại

NOVEL

HAS
SPRING
ALREADY
ARRIVED

Has spring already arrived

Trường Hà Vũ Toại

Novel
HAS SPRING
ALREADY ARRIVED

Edition 2
2024

Herstellung und Verlag:
BoD – Books on Demand, Norderstedt
ISBN: 9783758332128

Has spring already arrived

Author's words:

As usual, the author would like to point out that the content of the story collection is a product of the imagination.

All coincidences are outside the author's intention.

Therefore, the author assumes no responsibility for the contents of this story collection.

Author:

Vu Duy Toai,

Pseudonym:
Trường Hà Vũ Toại

Many thanks to the author's partner, Maria Vu Duy Thi Niem created the conditions for the author to complete this collection of stories.

Together with my children Yen-Ngan and Minh-Khoa, I am very touched by their support in completing the work.

I have dreamed of literature and art since my youth.

I would especially like to thank my children for allowing me to use their artwork as covers for my works, especially their paintings: Vu Nguyen Yen-Ngan, Vu Duy Minh Khoa,…

Trường Hà Vũ Toại

Has spring already arrived

HAS SPRING
ALREADY ARRIVED

Hearing the birds chirping like music to greet a warm, sunny morning behind the house, Ly rushed to the window and looked out. As Ly opened the two windows to let the morning warmth flow into Ly's room, he saw the full sun covering the branches and the adjacent garden.

The birds, including many sparrows, fly around before Ly's eyes, creating a vivid image.

Suddenly Ly wanted to sing, as if she wanted to absorb these wonderful scenes into her soul.

Ly remained silent, however, because when she looked down at the street from above, she saw an ashen gray car driving towards her house.

This car was unfamiliar to Ly because even though she tried to remember it, she still had no impression of it.

Then the car stopped right in front of Ly's house.

A man in his thirties and a woman in her thirties stepped out of the carriage, but

looks very nice.

Ly was startled when a strange guest came into the house. What's up. Who comes?

Looking for who?

Ly rushed downstairs and heard the noises and activity.

Greetings from her parents. Ly's brother's voice is the loudest, allowing him to hear every voice clearly:

- I greet you, aunt and uncle

- Is that Vinh? Well, you look more mature than before.

Vinh's laughing voice:

- Thank you, aunt, I wouldn't dare, you're still as young as you were back then.

- Oh, look, your son is not inferior to anyone else. Oh look, it's Ly, hey, he's really pretty.

Ly was still walking down the stairs when her parents hastily introduced:

- Say hello to Uncle and Aunt Lan.

- Hello, aunt and uncle.

Ly looked at the faces of the two people and was a little suspicious, she must have met them before.

Her mother's voice interrupted her thoughts:

- You didn't realize it was right. Uncle and Aunt Lan went to Saigon to work

That was ten years ago now.

My aunt and uncle used to visit our house occasionally, which is not surprising at all.

First, let's give you some rest.

The whole family then had lunch together.

During the meal, Ly saw her uncle and aunt Lan chatting happily with her parents.

Suddenly Aunt Lan asked her mother:

- By the way, how far is Ly studying now? Do you have a job?

- Lately he's been at home and helped me clean and cook, that's all.

Ly saw her aunt's eyes widen in surprise as she looked at her parents:

- Why don't you let him continue studying?

Only then did Ly see that her parents' faces were no longer happy. Ly's father spoke in a deep voice and quietly:

- My family situation is a bit bad, aunt, I have a nephew who helps me with housework so that I can finance school expenses.

Finally he just sighed and looked out into the yard.

There were a few little birds dancing.

Ly saw her aunt and uncle Lan looking sad after hearing her father's lament.

When I saw Uncle Lan with a glass of water in his mouth and never letting it go, he looked blankly at the sky. I don't know what he was calculating or thinking?

Actually, it's because Ly doesn't know much about her family's situation.

All I know is that Ly hasn't seen her mother as happy as before in more than half a year.

She didn't ask much because she saw that her parents were always whispering about their business, but never told Ly.

Ly's older brother Vinh is only worried about his performances.

Since he is an actor, his life is closely linked to the stage and the theater.

The money he earns helps him live an independent life. Ly's parents don't have to worry much about Vinh, because Ly once heard him say to her parents:

- Mom and Dad, don't worry about me, I have enough to live on.

However, Ly's parents are still worried about taking full care of her brother Vinh because as parents, no one will abandon their children even when they grow up.

Now, in front of Ly's aunt and uncle Lan, the matter is clearly revealed.

Her parents had had no luck doing business with people.

Ly greeted her parents, aunts and uncles, then retreated upstairs to bed and lay down to think so the adults downstairs could talk.

Ly never expected that this conversation would turn Ly's life into such an important turning point and change the life of a twenty-year-old girl.

That morning Lily woke up very early. It was a little over eight o'clock when Ly left the house.

Following her mother's instructions, Ly goes to the market street near Hoan-

Kiem lake ("Sword Lake") and then turns left a few hundred meters to reach a row of shops.

Mother carefully told Ly to enter the third store at the beginning of the street across from Ly's path.

There was a person wearing a brown shirt, holding a black stick, and wearing a hat with flowers and leaves, waiting for Ly.

Ly followed the directions to the location, the restaurant was crowded, so Ly hesitated.

The store has tables and chairs in the yard, so Ly doesn't know whether to go in or wait outside.

So Ly waited until the sun came up, then she was both depressed and disappointed.

Ly began to feel tired, accompanied by a growling in his stomach.

Still, Ly continued to wait to see if anyone would come to find her. Maybe people promised something and then gave up?

The shopkeeper just ran out and then came back into the shop with a look in his eyes like he was asking Ly if she needed to order something. The afternoon sun began to fade on the street in front of the store and the wind blew gently through Ly's hair. Ly suddenly felt a chill. As Ly looked up at the sky, he saw dark clouds gathering as if a storm was approaching.

She got discouraged, got up and decided to leave and go home and let history take its course. Ly thought to himself, nothing went wrong. The road ahead will certainly have many thorns.

(…)

Ly carefully followed her mother's instructions and went to the meeting point again. This time it's not the bar from last time. Ly arrived at the meeting point on a sunny afternoon, but it wasn't raining either. It was an Indian temple where Ly was taken and shown the way. At that time, visitors to the temple were not sparse, but not too crowded either. If it's just a matter of making an appointment, Ly says it's also ideal to find each other using predetermined signs.

Ly found a bench in the temple and gazed absently at the pilgrims performing ceremonies in the temple.

The smell of the ritual instruments wafted gently into Ly's nose.

Well, it's been an hour, why haven't we seen any news yet? Ly looked vaguely out the window, people were passing by, there were also old men and women, many boys and girls. Who will find Ly here? Old or young?

Ly continued to wait quietly.

The midday sunlight suddenly became bright for Ly. At that moment, Ly suddenly thought of the source that had led to the preparations for Ly's departure. Ly only vaguely knew that an acquaintance was being introduced, and from then on, Ly's aunt and uncle Lan were introduced.

It is said that Ly's uncle and aunt Lan also had difficulty learning about this introduction. Added to this is the price difference between the two sides. Ly once heard her mother telling the story that her uncle and aunt Lan said:

- You set the price too high, how can I afford it? The recommending party is a familiar place, so he also told the other party to give us a discount.

Ly's father is dreamy. The loss caused him to lose his usual cleverness and wisdom. So he had Ly's mother talk to Uncle Lan about the financial conditions and Ly's way out of Vietnam.

Mother said to Ly:

- You had to fly from Hanoi.

- Where are you going to fly, mom? Ly asked more.

- Looks like it's going to Europe.

Ly's mother answered Ly. At that time, Uncle Lan interjected:

- That's not it, sister. My niece will fly over the Russian capital first. The line then takes care of the pickup and the careful handling to the destination.

Ly's mother said casually:

- If they paid attention, they must be considerate.

A gust of wind blew into Ly's face, causing Ly to wake up.

Suddenly a young man passed by their place and looked at Ly with unusual eyes. Ly thought doubt-fully:

- Or is it my date?

But then that person left without looking back. Only then did Ly know he wasn't her date.

Ly was tired and got up to leave again.

At that moment Ly heard a voice saying to Ly:

- If you want something good, give it here.

Ly looked confused and saw an old man in his fifties walking with a cane.

Like a ghost, Ly looked him up and down intently. His head was covered with a hat made of all kinds of flowers.

He wore military robes like a monk; both his trousers and his shirt were brown.

Ly suddenly understood, realized who this person was, so she went over to give him a small package, inside was the gift her mother had told her.

He used a signal to talk to Ly.

After that, Ly went straight home, it was already after noon, Ly was worried about getting ready to cook because Ly's parents were away and Ly's stomach was growling after standing in the sun for several hours.

Recalling the meeting this morning, Ly was extremely nervous and worried because Ly knew that her mother had contacted and negotiated with a network that specialized in organizing people to go abroad to study to work.

The man Ly wanted to meet this morning was also a member of the organization that organized Ly's trip: when she gave this man her photo to make a passport book for a trip abroad, Ly stumbled and fell out of great worry as she was preceded by him.

The man in brown clothes held out a black stick for Ly to pick up. At this time, Ly didn't feel any pain, but saw the man's cold eyes. Ly reached out, touched the scratch on her knee and murmured:

- I've never been anywhere, I've been in danger, I don't know what will happen tomorrow?

Ly replayed the conversation with her parents that day about Ly's departure for Europe.

The organization's conditions are also attractive for Ly's parents: the travel organization only accepts money if Ly travels to a European country.

In return, her family had to pay a lot of money, but Ly herself didn't know how much.

The amount of money that enabled Ly to go abroad was largely borne by Uncle Lan.

Ly's parents no longer have money to care for Ly and go abroad to work.

People promise all sorts of things, namely going abroad to make money as a joke, and the money earned in some countries is calculated by "Dzu Ro" a silver million in Vietnam in less than a year.

Meanwhile, Ly's parents also need money to pay off their debts. They are Lan's aunt and uncle.

Ly also seems unable to help her parents pay off the debts, merely borrowing money so that her parents can take care of Ly and go abroad.

Ly was taken aback when she thought about living away from her parents and brother Vinh.

God, how can I bear this? Lily felt herself crying. I have to try to sacrifice work to earn money and help my parents.

But why doesn't Mr. Vinh help his family but only cares about dancing and singing? And who do parents owe money to?

What do your parents do or do?

Ly also knows that her father often receives well-dressed guests

Clothes, neat, straight clothes.

They talk to their father often

She only said a few sentences and then everyone walked out, leaving Ly unaware of her father's work.

Every day Ly saw that her parents were very secretive about business matters and therefore she was not allowed to ask anything.

Once, when Ly tried to ask her mother about the family situation when only mother and daughter were in the room, Ly only heard her mother say:

- We'll take care of it anyway.

And immediately after that came Mother's sigh, and at the same time Mother's eyes looked somewhere in the distance.

Ly followed her mother's eyes and saw only a room with many white clouds outside the small window. The wind gently moved the trees.

- If you have children helping parents, that's okay. Then Mother spoke gently to Ly.

When Ly saw this, she didn't want to get her mother in trouble.

Actually, Ly just dreams of continuing to learn like some of her friends. The dream of becoming my teacher

Ly is still in my head. If I were a teacher, I could still help my parents! Ly pursed his lips and sighed.

It's really wonderful to imagine the image of me standing on the podium for the children. This was Ly's dream since she was a child. Ly always quietly watched the teachers teach, imagining that they were fairies who came down from heaven to bring joy to the children of this earth.

But now I have to face the bitter reality.

Ly began to realize that it was not possible to live the life you wanted.

It depends on many other things. But we also have to find a way to achieve the goal we want, sometimes we get frustrated and stumble.

These thorns represent life's challenges. When she was in school, Ly heard her teachers teaching like this.

Now her parents and two parents need Ly's support, so a weak and small girl can only accept it. Ly and her parents got clothes to take with them on the trip to pave the way for the future this hybrid...

Ly's parents accompanied her to the airport the day Ly left the country.

It wasn't until more than ten days later that Ly found out her departure date. Even though it was early fall, it was still sunny.

The wind was blowing loudly, blowing everyone's hair.

The way to the airport seemed too short for Ly. She just wanted time to freeze so that her departure would be delayed, but that would only hurt her parents' work even more.

Ly believes so.

Her father looked at his daughter sympathetically and just sighed with short, repeated words:

- It's best to be very careful

- Yes.

When she arrived at the meeting point as instructed by the organization, Ly saw four other people standing with the guide.

Her mother told her he would go there with her.

The moment of separation was so sad.

Mom hugged Ly tightly and shed tears. She sobbed:

- Parents only hurt their children. Please understand your parents, child.

Ly hugged him tightly but then had to let go.

Ly saw her mother's red eyes, as if she were crying. A man with the task of showing the way approached the mother and daughter and said coldly:

- Here is your passport, we have to go.

Ly was still confused, when the people walking together looked at Ly, the man said quietly to Ly:

- The name in the book is another person. If asked, you must say your name... Remember it well, otherwise everything will be ruined.

Accordingly, Ly learned that the picture in the travel book or passport was Ly's, but the name was another person.

Ly still remembers Uncle Lan calling her father.

He just pursed his lips and said nothing more as he walked into the search area to weigh his suitcase and luggage.

Suddenly she turned to her mother and saw her buying bread for Ly to take with her.

Ly's mind was like a soulless person at this time. She absentmindedly hugged her mother again and whispered:

- Hello parents, you need to take care of your health.

The four people traveling together include two young men and the other two are young girls

The work seems much bigger than Ly. Since they weren't too worried, they seemed to feel very safe about this long journey.

Ly naturally feels closer to everyone than before.

The oldest young man looked at Ly, smiled and said:

- Don't worry, when you get there someone will greet you. All work is done.

Then he introduced himself:

- I'm Minh, we help each other.

Ly said hello too and didn't say anything else, just a quiet yes. Ly believes this could be a person in the organization, in a network that leads people to flee abroad. Because usually everyone has to take care of themselves and not pay much attention to others.

Especially if you have an organization that sends people abroad with full export documents, you need to know all the steps. I don't have enough energy to worry about it anymore, it tires my brain.

As Ly thought about this, she turned and looked behind the large hall of the airport, hoping to see her parents. These are Ly's two closest relatives in this world, but Ly never thought of leaving these two parents.

It's so ironic and ironic about life. People still say that life is inherently a destiny and no one can change it. How could Ly do anything else if everything was a fate preordained by God?

The airport is very crowded at the moment, people coming and going are crowding into the small area of the airport. Because of this, Ly could no longer see her parents. Suddenly Ly screamed softly in her mouth:

- Father, mother.

And then two tears flowed down Ly's burning cheeks.

After all the formalities were completed, the tour guide asked everyone to prepare to follow him to the boarding gate.

Ly blurted out:

- It is still early.

She still doesn't want to leave her parents. But he kept his head down and walked straight ahead. Ly waved goodbye to her parents and disappeared behind the airport security door.

Despite being Vietnamese when they were on the same flight, the people traveling with Ly didn't talk much during the trip. Ly was tired and could hardly sleep while Minh kept turning to watch Ly.

He planned to do everything for Ly, which surprised Ly.

Whenever the plane experienced a change in pressure, he would turn to Ly and tell her:

- Don't worry, the plane only flies low.

Ly closed his eyes tightly and dreamed. Even though she tried her best, Ly was still dizzy and sometimes felt like she was so disappointed that she went beyond her limits of tolerance. Ly thought to herself, maybe she hasn't been on a plane in a long time, so her body isn't used to altitude differences.

As Ly looked out the plane's small window, he saw dark clouds covering an area of the sky.

As Ly and the rest of the group of six got out and were about to leave the airport, the tour guide said:

- My mission here is over. I'll take you to someone to pick you up. The siblings will continue to be looked after by the program; the documents brought with you must be returned to the person collecting them.

Remember not to lose your papers

something bad happens.

Minh immediately asked:

- But we need papers to be able to live here later. Why give it to someone else?

- With so many questions, how do I know who has the answers?

I'm just a tiny part of the organization.

- Please don't ask. All I know is that in the future, if anyone asks for details about me, don't tell me, otherwise you will die and be driven back to the countryside or sent to prison.

- What do you mean?

- Oh, what's wrong, stupid question, I only have so much money, that's all I can say.

Then he left the airport and shook hands with a strange man.

When he saw this person, no one said anything because he was a Westerner with a thick beard and hair.

The eyes are bright but wild and cruel. Ly suddenly trembled as she thought about her future.

- Where is that? asked the voice of the girl accompanying Ly.

- This is the capital of Russia. Surely everyone has heard of Mat, right?

Nobody answered.

The Western man then greeted each person in Vietnamese, surprising and astonishing the entire group.

The pilot on the plane said a few words to the Westerner, then turned around and said:

- Now you follow the western man. I have completed my mission.

The Westerner picked up Ly's group in a small, dark-colored bus.

The car has lots of glass windows but with signs attached

It's sunny and when you get in the car you can't see everything outside.

The weather in the Russian capital was cool, even though it was midday.

Sunshine is rare as the sky is overcast and filled with gray clouds that appear to descend to the ground.

In the distance, the peaks of architecture can be seen from the rows of houses of all types, new, old and old.

The rows of houses are built in an ancient form with circular roofs with pointed peaks and the brick walls are mostly, or rather almost entirely, of red brick.

The images of red brick houses contrast with the blue background sky.

Ly suddenly exclaimed:

- Wow, that's strange.

Because Ly still hears Russia being described as a cold country in the northern hemisphere. I heard it's always cold. But now Ly feels completely different, the sky is sunny, blue clouds mix with white clouds, contrasting with the bright red villas.

Ly viewed Red Square as the place where the power of the former Soviet Union was concentrated, and now, in Ly's understanding, it is the center of the new Russian Federation, founded in the 1990s under the leadership of Russia.

Suddenly, alone in the car, Ly smiled because she remembered the story:

Not long ago, there was a famous tennis player who dared to fly a private plane alone and land right there. Red Square is a place where it is said to be extremely careful.

At that time, public opinion was loud because people could not understand how the air defense system of Russian airspace allowed foreign aircraft to enter such carefully protected airspace. It is true that in this world, under the sun, nothing is absolute.

Ly still remembers the plane pilot explaining that he wanted to become famous so that he could later enter politics.

History shows that Russia has long been a leading empire in a large, resource-rich region.

,Perhaps that is why Russia is rich in gold mines, diamonds, oil and gas mines and has unlimited power over the surrounding countries.

Ly saw some customers on the street wearing ba de xuy robes like in the international films she had seen during her time in Vietnam.

They walked along the river in the bright, golden sunlight

Against the color of the high-rise streets, the skyscrapers obscured the passing clouds.

Curiosity about the new world began to awaken in my mind.

But Ly woke up when he heard him speaking loudly in Vietnamese:

- Is anyone hungry? I'm pregnant

Bring bread and water for everyone.

Maybe it's because I ate on the plane

No one accepted the bread that the Western man offered. "Mr. Tay" added:

- We should have waited for another flight to arrive, but that flight was delayed, so let's go now.

So he turned the car around after loading the suitcases into the car. The car was driving on uneven roads so it swayed a lot, causing everyone in the car to overturn. There was no rain at that time, so the road was not so bad that it would be difficult for cars to move on.

After a while someone complained of nausea and wanted to vomit.

The old man handed the paper bags and shouted:

- Why are you so in love? Then his mouth murmured something that Ly couldn't hear clearly.

Ly thought to himself: These organizations took people's money and are still upset.

Since then, Ly simply remained silent and didn't dare to complain anymore.

Along Ly Street, looking at the trees on both sides of the street, there are many branches with bright yellow flowers that look like the golden sunlight at dawn.

The car drove for about half a day until it reached an area that resembled a small village. The car then drove on until it got a little dark and then entered a forest with lots of trees. Ly also heard the strange sounds of the animals living in the forest.

However, the car continued to roll. A few hours later it was raining quite heavily. The forest was dark and gloomy, the car's lights shone brightly on the road, clearly illuminating the white rain in front of the car.

Ly heard a few people in front of him talking to each other that they were about to reach the border. Ly couldn't hear the border, but only knew that people would have to get out of their cars and start walking again.

And then there was this moment: Ly and everyone had to get out of the car to continue walking, even though it was raining and the wind was blowing too hard, so Ly had to stay with the two women in the group.

The group continued hiking in the dark night with the tiny flashlight of the guide, who spoke Vietnamese.

After just a few kilometers, the road became uneven and the ground was both slippery and rocky, making noise when walking on it.

Suddenly a scream rang out in the empty night, causing the whole group to lose their souls and not understand anything. A Vietnamese voice rang out in the dark:

- Dead, miserable, someone fell into a hole in the street.

Then the leaders rushed to work to help the victims. The whole group was stopped in the middle of the night. The wind wasn't relatively as strong as when I got out of the car, but it was enough to make Ly shiver every time the wind blew. Ly stood hunched over.

First aid for falls in the middle of the street also takes a lot of time as the victim experiences shin pain and therefore requires temporary treatment.

One of the leaders asked everyone to remain calm.

- We continue.

Then he sighed:

- This part of the road rarely has holes. Why did I fall into such a hole today?

Mr. Ly's complaint was clearly heard, every word. There was a little anger in his voice about what happened tonight.

He also added that he was lucky that he was outside the dangerous area, otherwise it would have been too dangerous if there were wild animals and people.

He stretched out the three words, darling, sounding so sad. Nobody dared to think further.

In addition, if there are wild animals, no one can do anything at this time. That's what Ly thought to himself.

"Who dares to have the courage to jump out and face wild animals on a dark and lonely night like this?

Maybe he just said it like he was thinking about the people he was with. Maybe he was just thinking about the money he would win if the group reached a safe place."

Ly looked at the person who had fallen into the hole and injured his leg.

At this point it was already getting a little dusk, so you could still see around a little, although only very faintly.

Ly saw a few people walking to the branches on the side of the road as if they were looking for something.

According to people, they want to find a way to temporarily graft branches into the injured person's leg so that he can temporarily walk. but he complained of pain and could not move on his own.

Therefore, it was difficult to have two people carry it on their armpits.

The crowd had to stomp around because some people hurt their feet. Everyone groaned and sighed under the cold, foggy night in the distant clearing that had been imprinted on the sky. Surprisingly, someone in the group reported that they had brought a spray to cool the wound. The fact that the wound was cooled to prevent pain was a big help to him.

He no longer complains of pain.

So after about half an hour of rest the group continued on their way.

Seeing the group's hardships, Ly suddenly felt pain and cried out in her heart:

- Oh mom and dad, why do I suffer so much?

Then Ly prayed quietly for their arrival.

The raindrops subsided and the wind died down, so the group walked quite a distance and then found a place with a car to pick them up at dawn.

This newly picked up car has an ash gray color and looks new, so the car drives quite smoothly.

The car drove through the fields, leaving the deserted area and getting onto the smooth and level road, so that the whole group seemed to breathe a collective sigh of relief.

The person with the injured leg is still silent. Maybe she's trying to suppress the pain, or she's been given more cooling medication to ease the pain.

Ly wanted to look back at the forest she had walked through, but she could only see it dimly.

Then the car rolled smoothly along the asphalt road and gradually passed through populated areas.

When he looked through driver Ly's windshield, all he saw were a few scattered one-story houses and passing farms. The car swayed for almost half an hour and then stopped. Ly was extremely happy because it was more than she could bear.

Now I'm hungry and thirsty.

When the car stopped in front of an old two-story house in a sparsely populated area, it was already dusk.

Ly's eyes no longer had the strength to take in more of the scene around her.

I'm so tired, my eyelids are heavy and I just want to sleep deeply and soundly like at home on the soft bed.

As he entered the house with a group of Vietnamese accompanying Ly, he saw two people come out of the house to greet him, a man and a woman who were already quite old.

As Ly listened to the exchange and conversation between the two sides, he knew that this was a temporary inn to stay overnight so that he would continue on to the Czech side the next morning, from Ly's understanding it was the Czech Republic.

Two people go to each room and the bathroom is shared.

The man in the house, whose name was Uncle Sau, raised his voice as if he wanted everyone to hear:

- Everyone agreed to serve dinner together in half an hour.

When they heard this, everyone was very excited. Having a hot meal was a dream after a long journey of several days in prison, so why wouldn't you want that?

Ly took a quick shower and changed. When she was finished, she went to eat and saw bread on the table.

Oh my god, bread, cold cuts and fried rice with sausage again.

It's okay, Ly went in to eat but felt restless and confused.

During the meal, Ly received six uncles

said that the next day the trip was to Czechoslovakia and traveled by train and minibus.

As we approach the Czech capital, we will be split into two groups, with each side taking a different direction based on the organization's agreement with the people traveling in the group.

Ly dared to ask Uncle Sau:

- Uncle Six, do you have a job there?

- Probably yes, if it was handed over, it must be like that.

What is handover? Ly didn't understand anything, but Uncle Sau was absentmindedly taking medication

The leaves are smoked and the smoke is released to fly high as if she is using her dream to merge it into nothingness.

That night, Ly was woken up by strange noises, so she couldn't sleep.

The house is on the edge of the suburban forest, so a lot of noises from insects, owls, etc. can be heard.

She misses her home, misses her parents, uncles and aunt Vinh, what is everyone doing now? I probably think about Ly a lot because everyone is getting ready to celebrate Tet.

Spring returns home, but Ly is absent. Now Ly is alone in a foreign country. Ly will welcome spring in a land where even the Ly family doesn't know a single word.

She went because she wanted to give her family, Ly's parents and brothers a cozy spring. Tomorrow they can welcome spring again without having to worry or be sad about life's difficulties.

Ly put her hand on her forehead and whispered: Spring will come...

As the car left the area with homes and rows of trees on either side of the road, the sky was just getting dark, so the scene began to fade before Ly's eyes.

There are now 6 people in the car, including Ly.

Ly noticed that the people with her were all sitting quietly with their eyes closed. Ly wasn't sure whether they were sleeping or closing their eyes and dreaming of the life of tomorrow, which Ly also found as colorful as humanity's spring. .

The silence in the car was as overwhelming as the darkness outside, making Ly feel as if everything had stopped. The uneven dirt road causes the vehicle to sway up and down, sometimes causing people to pile into each other.

Some people on the bus sighed, others roared with joy, giving Ly a headache.

The man continued talking:

- I don't know when I can stop the car to rest. I'm so tired, aren't I?

Ly remained silent and didn't answer, but pretended to close her eyes as if she didn't hear anything.

Ly felt that the man who said the above sentence thought he was going on a trip?

Ly's mood was once again the same confusion as when she first got off the plane.

Just then the car stopped, in the darkness of the night Ly gave up because she couldn't see anything, only heard the driver's car door slamming and then indistinct people talking. Shots. Then a flashlight shone through the windshield of the car, the shuffling brought it back to Ly's ears, and the sound of banging against the wall of the car stunned Ly.

However, the driver then returned to the car.

His expression in the dark night was as cold as night dew. He quietly took out his cigarette. A man standing next to the lighter lit a cigarette and said something to him.

The man answered loudly, puffing on his cigarette. Cigarette smoke flew into the car and caused several people to cough. The man took a quick look inside the car, smoked out his cigarette and started the engine to continue driving.

Ly breathed a sigh of relief.

She prayed silently.

- Oh my god, it's really a scene where you're miles close to a girl!

Thinking about the two girls riding on the same bus, Ly felt her heart clench. Ly looked through the small window and saw the twinkling stars at night.

It's winter in Russia now, there are no clouds, so it's probably colder than when it's cloudy and windy.

As Ly thought about Russia, he suddenly thought of the image of the emperors of Russia in the past before the Red Army took over the government.

She reflects on the days of the Soviet era with communist ty-coons like Stalin, to whom Vietnamese communist suppor-ters offered ridiculously thoughtful verses as a poet of Vietnamese stature.

On the day the Red Army took over Russia, Emperor Nicholas' entire family was killed. It is said that a princess fled to France. Now that Russia has seceded from communism, if she is still alive, she will return to visit her family's grave.

"Family".

When we think of those who died in the Soviet era, Ly notes that these honors have no meaning at all, but also contain bitter irony towards the souls of the victims.

Ly thinks about people, in fact there are many strange points, because poetry is a symbol of human love, emotional vibrations from the heart full of love, but people write poems about the torment and torture of children. People, things that have broken people's hearts.

Ly is a person who is very interested in culture and history, so she admires heroes in history books. She had the idea of becoming a teacher. If her wish is granted, Ly will follow history and culture in general.

Thinking about standing on the school podium as a young teacher, Ly smiled softly. Then life will certainly be very, very interesting. But not everyone gets what they want.

At this point, Ly suddenly remembered that Ly's brother is making a film about love in a certain part of Vietnam, her heart is also pounding and she smiles slightly.

She just wanted her brother to succeed so he wouldn't have to leave like her.

But right after that, Ly suddenly felt that her mind was dark. She trembled slightly as she looked around her surroundings. Ly was uneasy about the thoughts that had just crossed her mind.

If everything in this world could easily turn out the way you want, this world would be a paradise or a heavenly place.

In the darkness of the night, the sounds of owls could be heard again and again in the groves along the roadside.

Ly breathed lightly and listened to people saying that the owl's cry signaled a good omen, but according to Ly, the owl had scary eyes and was sometimes carefree.

That's why they say it's an owl's eye.

The stars still followed her, still in the sky as she lost her thoughts.

Ly was also surprised to see that the two women traveling together did not talk or ask questions.

Maybe they are too tired or shy around the strange men in the car.

They also looked emaciated and listless, as if they had exhausted their strength on this arduous journey.

The car suddenly rocked violently and then slowed down.

The sun's rays in the direction of the car penetrated deep inside and blinded Ly a little. It turned out that the car then turned onto an empty street with trees and stopped in front of a large mansion-style house.

The old house was whitewashed in faded white, there were many layers of moss on the wall, and green branches stuck to the wall.

The four sides of the house are large areas with only two or three medium-sized trees, providing enough shade for passing guests who want to rest, drink a glass of water or smoke a cigarette and then get on with their lives.

Ly suspected that someone wanted to take away her need for privacy, so she didn't pay attention to it, because Ly was also very lazy, her throat felt dry after a long journey.

Suddenly the Western driver spoke in a foreign language to the Vietnamese sharing the car, then Ly heard him say again in Vietnamese:

- Now let's take a break to eat. Maybe we should leave right after dinner because tomorrow the road will be slippery and we can't walk fast.

"Oh, another Westerner who speaks Vietnamese.

Why are they so talented?

Vietnamese is difficult for me to learn."

As Ly thought about this, he suddenly felt brave and asked:

- Where are we going?

- This man went into the house and answered in the sound of the wind:

- Let's go to the Czech Republic.

- Where is this Czech Republic?

Ly wanted to know, but the man accompanying her replied as if he knew Ly's thoughts:

- The Czech Republic, also called Czechoslovakia at the time, is a country next to Poland. From Poland we will have many directions.

The sound of the loud wind was heard, creating the sound of the man suffering, diluting the man's voice and making Ly unable to hear clearly.

Then as the wind passed, Ly heard his voice:

- Anyway, we are going to an area where Vietnamese live and do wholesale business, it is easier for us to manage and we can have the food we need.

"Everyone has needs, including you, right?"

When Ly heard him say that, he was also a little excited inside.

No matter what, who doesn't need little things for a long trip?

Ly told herself the things she really needed and hoped that she would have a chance to buy them to use them.

The sky was full of dark clouds, so the wind blew quite strongly, bringing cold to people's hearts, so Ly just exclaimed softly and quickly went into the house:

- Yes

Suddenly Minh turned around and said to Ly:

- Hey lady, the Czech Republic is also called the Czech Republic. It used to be called Czechoslovakia, but it was divided into two countries, leaving the only name left which is the Czech Republic. Have you got it yet?

Li nodded slightly. She didn't answer, having heard the explanation before. However, Ly also secretly felt that Minh was really a kind-hearted person.

Everyone got bread and a small bowl of porridge with some chicken. Ly swallowed some hot chicken porridge and felt light.

She knew chicken porridge would help with a cold, so she finished the bowl of ginger-flavored porridge. And in fact, ginger is a good remedy for protecting the body, especially against colds and colds. Ly remembers her mother always saying that. So if someone in the house has a cold, Ly's mother immediately cooks a pot of chicken porridge with lots of ginger. She forced her to eat so that she would immediately recover from her cold by sweating.

Ly realizes that the chicken at home is delicious, but the chicken here is so wasteful.

She didn't feel appetizing at all, but eventually finished the bowl of hot chicken porridge. The fragrant scent of ginger makes Ly crave a piece of ginger jam.

"I wish I could eat a piece of ginger jam, that would be great."

The food is acceptable but the sleeping area is really terrible, especially for a girl like Ly.

Well, there's nothing I can do about it as long as I get there and tell her parents the news so they don't worry too much.

After two or three days of driving, Ly and everyone had to walk through the forest that evening.

According to the guidebook, we would have to wade through a small stream to cross the border

But the weather was cold and the wind was blowing quite strongly, so the steps were hesitant and shaky at night because everyone was too tired after days of drifting.

Especially the forest paths, where the grass grows almost over the pedestrian's shoulders.

Westerners are tall, so they can see the road clearly and walk quickly.

Only the following group of people encountered obstacles with overgrown grass on the way.

The journey had to be stopped countless times as one person after another stopped for a variety of reasons.

Excessive tiredness is also possible, thirst is the most common reason and not the last, but the need to go to the toilet. A reason that everyone knows.

"In fact, crossing the creek is still the best route because it escapes the control of the Border Patrol," said the son, who traveled with Ly, as he sat and applied oil to the swelling caused by insects in the forest.

Ly wondered why this guy, Minh, was so knowledgeable about moving.

Or is he in the organization? It's terrible. Ly thought as he walked.

Finally, Ly and everyone else arrived in the Czech Republic on a clear and cloudy morning

The car carried people who didn't have much breath left to look at the long streets with tall trees, colorful flowers and rows of houses with many winding hills and mountains, surrounded by open forests and dense forests. They took Ly to a crowded area. The driver spoke up as if he wanted to answer the passengers' questions:

- We will visit a Vietnamese market called Sapa Market in the Czech capital Prague. Ly tried to recognize the name of the city because this was the first time she had gone abroad and also the first time she had come to this place, a place completely foreign to Ly.

Apparently there was an agreement or agreement in advance so that the group went straight to the market with acquaintances of the people who owned shops.

Ly saw a middle-aged man with a fairly fit physique come out to greet everyone. Through their exchange, they introduced Ly to the man who, as Ly had predicted, was the owner of a shop in the market.

The shopkeeper called out another person from inside. It was a young woman with a small figure:

- Hello, brothers and sisters.

The shop owner introduced Ly to the other woman, through whom Ly knew she was his wife. After we discussed and exchanged ideas, the shopkeeper said to Ly:

- Don't be shy at all. Let's just see each other as sisters and family.

She looked directly at Ly and continued:

- I'll take care of the shop here and give you a hand. Sales work is also easy.

Ly heard her say and smiled brightly, making her feel comfortable too. Ly replied shyly:

- Yes, I will try it.

After saying that, Ly looked up at the front of the stand. On the other side of the market there is a street with two rows of green trees on the side of the road.

At this point the sunlight still remained on the trees, a cool breeze blowing through and blowing through Ly's hair.

Through the introduction of the men who brought Ly to this market, Ly was given the task of running a store that sold clothing and other sundries.

Then they continued with two girls in the same group. Ly didn't know where they were going, only saw two young girls turning around and waving at Ly with sad sunset eyes. Ly was also sad when she had to say goodbye to her two companions for a while, but also brings with her many memories.

The boy also waved goodbye to Ly. As for the guides, each had a cigarette dangling from his lips and walked straight ahead without turning to look at Ly.

Ly came here for the first time and was very surprised by the hustle and bustle of activity. Who are the buyers and who are the sellers with deafening shouts at the stalls evenly distributed throughout the market? Ly noted that the customers were foreigners of all kinds.

They come to this market in groups and groups. Then Ly saw buses full of passengers.

When their bus pulled into the bus station, people got out, quickly went to the market and talked loudly, disturbing the entire shopping area.

Ly thought for a while and thought to himself who is the owner of this shopping area in Czechoslovakia when all the

Vietnamese shops are together. How do they come together and live such a busy life?

Ly heard Western and Vietnamese men in the group of guides and drivers talking. Some were smoking cigarettes, others were holding glasses of beer and gulping down drinks as if they were dying of thirst.

Lily felt extremely bored. They seemed to want to completely forget about Ly and the people in the group who came here after a long and arduous journey.

The big man told everyone:

- From now on my duty is fulfilled. It's my job to get everyone here, and what happens next is up to you.

She informed her family to settle the balance. Thanks in advance.

If the organization is not considerate, please have compassion.

Hearing this, Ly was confused and wanted to ask, but the man turned away with his cigarette still on his lips and blew the smoke back to the wrong side, where Ly stood speechless in the wind, feeling infinite sadness. They organize and promise high paying jobs, now working in such a rudimentary place is a scam.

Ly could see her anger rising within her, but she couldn't do anything about it, especially not about the stereotypes of the man smoking a cigarette with a beer bottle in his hand.

The working days went by so quickly that it has been three months since Ly arrived in Czechoslovakia.

Ly called her parents back to Vietnam and since her arrival in the Czech Republic she has regularly written letters and called her family back to Vietnam.

The news of her parents and older brother made Ly very excited to continue her days in this cold Czech land.

Ly's brother kept wanting to arrange a meeting with his sister, but Ly couldn't carry out his plan even though she still wanted her brother to come here. It's easy to say, but the whole journey is full of thorns and traps, sometimes you have to pay with your whole life.

Even though Vietnamese people came to Sapa Market in large numbers and from all different places, Ly still felt that something was missing from life.

Little by little, Ly got to know the sisters and friends and became friends, so that Ly often confided in them.

Thao is Ly's closest relative.

Through Ly's words, Thao said a sentence that Ly heard coldly everywhere:

- You're lonely, Ly.

Ly turned her face away to look at the sunset sky through the small window in her motel room.

The color of the sky is red and yellow, as if Ly's heart is playing with it.

Maybe Thao is right, I really am lonely.

- Oh yes, I miss my parents. You guessed correctly.

- Come on, I'm here, hello, don't think you can lie to me. Or find you.

In the days that followed, Ly and Thao often went shopping together on the Czech capital's main street, which street vendors called Czech.

The streets here have long been a place that attracts many tourists from far away.

Especially after the disintegration of Eastern Europe, the number of visitors from Western Europe, Asia and America is increasing day by day.

Gradually, the Czech capital became an international crime hub, as Ly had once read.

Recently Thao also talked a lot about this Czech country, it is so full of people who are as happy as Tet,

Thao always said that loudly. But Ly is not very enthusiastic about this European life.

Completely alien.

People are much colder than in Vietnam. Ly thought this as he left with Thao.

As for Thao, she is completely careless and does not pay attention to the ideas in Ly's head, which are expressed in indifference and indifference to the streets, but Ly walks slowly.

Thao pulled Ly's hand:

- I went across the street to eat this strange but delicious dish.

- Where what?

- Follow me and you will know.

Thao took Ly to a small restaurant on an empty street corner. After deciding on the dish, the two called someone to order drinks.

- Why is it so hot today?

As she complained, Ly raised her hand to wipe her forehead.

During the meal, Thao Ly told many stories about crossing the border and other forest crossings of people who went abroad like Ly.

Thao said they had to pay a lot of money but couldn't get through because they were too strictly controlled and monitored.

The Border Patrol now has an infrared tracking system so they can clearly see people running through the woods in the dark.

- You see it like daytime, Ly.

Lily rolled her eyes but didn't say a word. She couldn't even drink a sip of water. Thao continued:

- There was a girl who came to Germany, she was dumped on the street alone, and then she had trouble finding her way, she was tricked into becoming pregnant.

- Why can that be so?

- Well, our Vietnamese people already live peacefully, so they don't need it.

They just like to satisfy their intentions.

They say they help, but they all involve buying and selling.

Huh, it is convenient to buy and sell. After completing their work, they find a way to release them to a specific location where they are sent to a camp for at least six months or longer.

Everything is too late. With the ...

At this point, Thao took a sip of water. A bird flew across the sky in front of two people who confided in each other.

The sun shines on the gray tiled roofs.

There were a lot of people passing by, but it still wasn't too loud.

Thao continued:

Hey, I heard that a lot of people have set up lines to bring people to England.

- I don't understand why I have to go to England?

- But is it running smoothly?

- They drove to the pier and then postponed the trip to wait for the time.

- Waiting period?

- Then wait for the opportunity. Whenever the opportunity arises to cross the river and sea, they take it immediately.

- What's the chance, Thao?

Thao rolled his eyes:

- Oh my God, all kinds of ways, all kinds of tricks.

- ...

- I heard that some people broke off the keys from trucks with cars and put dozens of people in there.

When the truck arrived in England everyone jumped down and it seemed like everything had gone smoothly.

So I have to give money to the leaders hahaha... a miserable life, getting to a place like Britain is considered a waste of money because this side has almost no control and therefore it is easy to live underground. I can live illegally Every day I work illegally, earn money to pay off debts and send money to Vietnam to my family and relatives.

The only problem is where the money will come from and how long it will take to pay off such a large debt.

As Ly looked at the couple helping each other and passing in front of her, she sighed softly:

- But it seems like not everyone is like that, Thao?

- Ah, so... what does that mean, Ly?

Please tell me clearly and clearly.

- Then everyone has their own way of cracking it.

- Yes, I heard that it is safe to sit with the driver when going to level 3 or higher

The driver ran straight across the border with fake documents, but passed.

- What is Level 3, Thao?

- Depending on the level, i.e. depending on the entry price.

At the lowest price it is only a few thousand green coins.

What do you call grass, so cheap as grass?

- God, a few thousand green money said it was cheap!

Ly howled, causing the guests to look at Ly and Thao in awe.

They thought the two were arguing.

An old woman sitting in the corner of the shop looked at the two shyly, sighed and turned around to say something to the waiter. He looked at the two of them and went back to work. Ly was speechless. Thao withdrew Ly:

- That's it, the size of a dozen is large, not huge.

When you become a huge man, it's over twenty.

- Wow, where does so much money come from?

- Oh, hey, don't you really know?

The mandarin's son also quickly escapes.

Just go as best you can. Living without a shadow of tomorrow, why stay there, people say this and that country to console themselves when they are trying to hold on but live for themselves or for their children... that is the problem. This is Ly.

Suddenly Ly saw a Czech police patrol car pull up in front of the restaurant.

Two police officers got out of the car.

Ly panicked when she saw them approaching the front door of the store.

Thao turned around, followed Ly's gaze and said quietly:

- You do not have to be scared. They have already passed.

Tired, Ly stopped eating and asked to go home. As they left the restaurant, Ly tried to follow every move of the two police officers who were walking in the opposite direction of her friends Thao and Ly.

The sun was still calmly shining yellow stripes on the street of the noisy district, as if it didn't care about Ly's fear.

Suddenly, Thao's eyes looked intently across the street. Ly was startled and looked into Thao's eyes.

Oh look, a Vietnamese girl is right, she's walking confused up and down the street at the intersection opposite the restaurant where Thao and Ly are sitting. Thao stood up:

- Honey, we have to see if the girl can help her.

- Naturally.

Ly spoke a few words of approval to Thao.

The two said a few words to give the money to the shopkeeper, and then ran together to the young girl's apartment.

Ly and Thao ran and shouted to the girl walking on the street. The girl didn't seem to know someone was calling her, so she walked quickly in the hot sunlight. Thao had to try to shout loud enough for the other girl to hear. Eventually Ly and Thao caught up with the other girl.

After exchanging news on both sides for a while, all three people returned to the store.

Thao pulled out a chair so the other girl could sit. After confessing that her name was Lan, Thao immediately asked:

- Where are you going? Where do you come from?

The girl named Lan was brushing the stray hair from her sweaty face and answered quietly:

- I came here from Germany, sisters.

- Oh, why, why are you from Germany? What does that mean ?

Lan breathes:

- I have a child, sister. I sent my children here from Germany for business reasons.

- Oh, I have a baby. How ? Why ? We want to go to Germany, but why did Lan come here from Germany?

- Let me tell you two.

In fact, when I went to Russia everything went smoothly, sisters, it was just suffering during the journey from Russia through the forest to Poland and then through Czechoslovakia, and then I would give up in any other country, I don't remember. Hey, sister.

- Poor girls died on the shore on the way here.

- How are you, Lan?

"Women and girls, you know, as a woman, I can't bear the long journey, so I get sick, but I can't be saved, I can't help it, I'm just waiting to die."

- How's the ending, Lan?

Ly asked.

Lan continued:

- When we went with three girls, two died, and when the third was seriously ill, I kept begging for her life, but she kept having asthma attacks, I think it was because of the sacred forest. Poisonous water, sisters, it makes it impossible to breathe.

Lan paused for a moment because she was choking, then said again to Thao and Ly:

- When the unfortunate girl was suffocated, the whole crowd was confused, some people gave her a bottle of wind oil to apply, some people administered lime tablets, as if expecting a miracle to happen to their companions. But then the girl sighed and turned her head to say goodbye to the attic.

A small funeral was celebrated in the dark of night with the song of owls and the gentle drops of rain falling in the wild ancient forest on the European border.

Those who attended the funeral were the ones who had been with the villain, so everyone was sad about her powers.

The funeral was silent, not even the sound of wild animals in the distance and the sound of owls.

Through the dim, cloud-covered moonlight, Lan saw some people folding their hands and making other signs consistent with their faith.

Some people sat on the ground, their hands holding their heads and their shoulders shaking violently. Surely everyone thinks to themselves that they do not know when they will arrive, or that they will have to bury their bodies in a foreign country, in the jungle, where no one knows.

Otherwise it's just silence mixing with the night.

Finally, a cross was placed on the grave because it is a symbol of peace. It is unclear what religion the deceased belonged to, but regardless, the cross would have been a sign of where the victim was buried.

In this silence, Lan suddenly heard a noise that was reminiscent of the sound of trees touching each other, growing louder and louder.

Everyone was silent so they didn't notice the heavy rain that had just come.

The rain came so suddenly that no one could resist it, so they had to be hit by the rain and soaked all their clothes. Everyone was shaking, but they still had to go.

Suddenly a young man came up to Lan, gave her a raincoat and said:

- Use this coat to avoid getting cold. Anyway, it's all wet.

Lan seemed a little hesitant, then the young man said calmly to Lan:

- It's Okay, I'm used to being wet and cold. She just got sick and probably won't last.

Then he spoke again, as if pleading with Lan:

- Take it and put it on, miss.

Lan saw that the young man's attitude towards her was so considerate that she was touched, so she reached out to take the raincoat from the hand of the young man she never knew. As he handed over the shirt, Lan's eyes met the young man's gentle eyes.

Lan whispered:

"This is why we know that not all people in this world are the same"

Then Lan continued to talk about her trip in a very tired voice. Perhaps the journey from Germany to Czechoslovakia was too difficult for Lan.

After traveling for half a month and arriving in Europe, Lan believed she would be fine, probably only having a few days or weeks left to get there. At that time, Lan will tell her family back home the good news.

Unexpectedly, yes, no one expected, Lan suddenly felt a headache and dizziness one night. She coughed nonstop, so one of them said:

- I have medicine here. If you take it, it will give you instant relief.

The voice of the person administering the medicine was hoarse and muffled, which made Lan feel guilty.

Although Lan was exhausted, she was also very scared, she had to be careful.

How can you trust anyone here? She swallowed, took a deep breath, and calmed down for a while, refusing to take the pill.

The car drove endlessly through the uneven forest, up and down.

The wind was not very strong, but the forest trees swayed in the darkness. Occasionally a wild animal will quickly run out of the car's headlights. After a few quiet hours, Lan started coughing again. "Very hard," Lan said, so this time Lan didn't need to think or hesitate at all, she took the pill and drank it with a bottle of water that the guide had given Lan to take the medicine. Only about five or ten minutes Later, Lan was stunned, thrilled, and fell asleep in the middle of the night. It seemed as if there was a clap of thunder that heralded the rain. When Lan woke up, she was lying in a room in a house in the middle of the forest.

This is the home of forest workers who stay overnight on busy work days, so according to the reports of those who passed by, the house is almost deserted. Lan was stunned to see that her body was in shock, her clothes were so tattered that they didn't cover her body as much. It was obvious that she had previously dressed very conservatively. Why are things like this now? In a panic, Lan shouted:

- Oh my God, what have you done to me?

None of the people accompanying Lan answered her.

The men in the tour group sat huddled together, smoking, puffing cigarette smoke into the sky, and looking up at the sky as if counting scattered stars. Nobody said a single word.

Lan said, half screaming, half pleading:

- Please let me know how it ends.

A young man once spoke to Lan during a trip to Lan:

- I'm sleeping soundly, girl, I really don't understand anything.

Lan rushed over to another young man, but he wasn't Vietnamese, so he just looked at Lan, sighed softly, and then turned in another direction to look at him, which made Lan even angrier.

Clouds gathered at night in the area of the lonely house in the middle of the forest. The wind whistled through the trees as if a group of snakes were crawling closer to the house.

They all threw cigarette butts on the ground.

Each person took a sip of water, and Lan was shocked by the bitter looks from those walking in the same group as Lan.

As soon as Lan mentioned this, she breathed quickly.

Lan's tears flowed down her cheeks, everyone lowered their heads crying, the pain of being a long-distance girl who had to leave her home.

Anyone who hears the story of a girl named Lan clearly understands what happened that night in the abandoned house in the middle of the jungle in the stormy wind and rain.

The howls and screams of wild animals don't sound as pitiful as the gasps of brutal violence of humanoid animals in the darkness of the night. A fight, a duel in which the separation of victory and defeat was too obvious.

Finally, there is the silence of suffering with the moans of a woman in the middle of the night forest.Lan sat sobbing, her shoulders shaking.It was slowly approaching late Afternoon. The restaurant was full of people coming in and out, and it became even busier and louder than when Lan entered the restaurant. The colored lights of the billboard hanging on the roof of the store lit up Lan's pale face. In any case, Lan's expression was less sad than before.Then Lan continued with a tired breath:- Later, when I arrived in Germany, I wandered here and there and finally met a Vietnamese man who had been living in Germany for a long time and was willing to let me in to bring a temporary home to sort out my future life.

Not long after, I became pregnant. My sister worked feverishly to help me until the day of birth.

After the birth I stayed there for about three months.

Suddenly one day my girlfriend came home and told me to pack up all my clothes and belongings and follow her to the car. Next she drove me far away. I fell asleep, holding the baby in my arms and asked:

- Where are you taking me?

- No more, go to the orphanage.

Then she laughed loudly.

- No, I'll take you to the temple. There are many good people there who will help you, Lan.

The conversation between Lan, Thao and Ly was suddenly interrupted by noise, then by the noise outside the door of the restaurant where the three were sitting and confiding in each other. Then people were talking and dogs were barking. When you looked outside, it turned out to be a group of people protesting. They walked in rows of five or six people in a fairly orderly line and there were people holding loudspeakers, banners and hand-held posters, but Lan, Ly and Thao didn't understand anything, just assumed that they were doing something. demand something that is part of their rights.

- This is a free country. Everyone has the right to stand up for their interests. Thao said so. Ly nodded and looked absentmindedly at the ceiling of the restaurant, without further criticism. Lan had a sad face and just looked at the protest group in the light May rain. The fact is that there were also police officers in the protest group and all three were shocked when they saw them following the booing group. Then everything was over after only about ten minutes over. The light rain has stopped and the sun is slowly shining on the road surface, even if it is just a hint, it is enough to inspire more confidence for life tomorrow.

Lan continued to tell her story. It took a long time for the car to reach the temple, which was far away on the outskirts of a major German city.

The car drove over many roads through many provinces from central Germany to northern Germany and therefore had to overcome many hills and plains. So sometimes the car goes too fast, sometimes it's slow, and sometimes it has to brake quickly, making the occupants dizzy and tired.

So while driving, your sister Lan told a story about the German city so that she would be less sleepy and overcome her motion sickness.

As the car drove through the winding rivers, the driver continuously told stories about these wonderful places in Germany.

Lan also heard Ms. Hoa tell stories of people who came to Germany and also lived very successfully there.

Despite Hoa's words, Lan still hung her head, her hair hanging down, showing an attitude of being too tired and car sick.

Suddenly Lan exclaimed:

- You stop the car, I'm so dizzy, I can't take it anymore, sister.

When Hoa saw this, he tried to advise Lan:

- Maybe walk a few more kilometers, then we'll stop at the gas station, I'll give you something to drink and your tiredness will disappear.

Ms. Hoa is a driver, but always awake, from the beginning to now there is no sign of tiredness on the way, she tried her best to explain to Lan:

- You know, during the war this city was almost completely destroyed. After Peace Day, people used all their strength to rebuild and build a new life.

The car left the highway and traveled along streets smaller than the highway. It meandered for about fifteen minutes before arriving at the temple with three main attractions.

After going to the temple and learning about Lan's situation through the words of Mrs. Hoa, whom she knew here, Lan was taken to her house by an old lady to live there and take care of her young children. She lived alone and therefore often went to the temple to perform meritorious deeds. When Ms. Lan saw Lan's situation, she was very touched.

The temple was empty that day, so the old woman had time to hear Lan's story clearly.

After hearing this, she quietly went to the main hall to light incense and pray silently.

The smell of incense sticks wafted into Lan's nose, she was excited, a little dizzy, and she staggered, which startled her friend.

As she looks out onto the street from the main hall, the symbolic flag of Buddhism in five colors on the flagpole flutters in the strong wind.

At the top of the flagpole, tufts of white clouds passed like thick fog, playing with the wind.

- Oh no, I must have been hit by the wind.

Lan was then helped by two people into a small room behind the main hall. On the way to the room, Lan vaguely saw the altar with pictures of many people. After their death, these people were entrusted here by their family members. On the altar, incense burns in a gilded copper urn that is polished to a very shiny shine.

Lan suddenly thought of her companion's grave without incense or smoke.

A person's life is so short that he has to endure so many hardships. Lan felt sorry for the fate of women in this world.

She sighed and followed the old woman.

Her head was still dizzy, so Lan had to lean on Ms. Hoa's body as she moved into the room, just off the main hall, a small, boring hallway painted and hung with yellow curtains.

Ms. Hoa spoke first:

- Or let me give you some wind.

Mrs. Hoa asked the old lady for a bottle of oil to tickle the tiger's name and started flirting with Lan with a coin.

Lan tried to endure the pain, but still let out a small groan as loud voices were heard outside the main hall. The old lady said quietly to the two of them:

- This is the group that says prayers at lunchtime. They come to perform the rituals and then help with the temple work.

The old woman looked at Lan, sighed, and motioned for her to lie down and rest peacefully.

It was pouring rain outside, the sound of the falling rain could be heard on the roof of the pagoda, the wind blowing into the small room made Lan shiver. Grandma said:

- As a girl I was also very aggressive, youth was enthusiastic, now I have a hundred things in my heart and head.

I also have children who have grandchildren the same age as you, but each of them has their own destiny. No one can escape the fate of heaven, Buddha.

The old woman Buddha's voice made Lan hear the sound of prayers and the sound of the pagoda bamboo sticks in the main hall. The thought of hiking brought

Lan back into the flow of thoughts of the past few months.

Fate was not lucky for Lan to meet Mrs. Hoa, an old lady in the temple who was cared for and cared for. Lan suddenly sobbed with emotion, her shoulders shaking and her face drooping, she sobbed like a child.

Lan cried for a while, then Mrs. Hoa said she had to go home, got up and slowly walked to the temple gate to say goodbye to Lan and the old lady.

It began to rain and dark clouds spread across the sky, making Lan think of her bleak future and the shadow of the clouds in the sky.

The old lady was really nice, even though she was old and not in good health, she helped a girl who was the same age as her children and grandchildren.

The old lady made Lan stay in the temple for a long time, waiting for the day when the flower bloomed.

At the temple, Lan helps the old woman with scripture work every day, and cooks vegetarian rice for the temple to sell to pay for the temple, and uses the money for the temple to help places in need.

Lan's cooking skills developed so quickly that the chefs praised Lan's skills. A nun even told Lan the following in the temple kitchen:

- After the deadline, you can open a restaurant. It is a very popular vegetarian restaurant.

When Lan heard this, she could only smile and say thank you. The days ahead are truly limitless.

After the birth, Lan was sad, but everyone in the temple comforted her and gave her advice. There was a nun who even tried to tell Lan a funny story and then everyone laughed, which also helped Lan ease her sadness.

At that time, Lan also had the idea of opening a restaurant in the future. But everything has to have its order, processes and time, Lan also thinks.

In addition, some capital is also required. It is not easy!

During the confinement period, Lan was enthusiastically cared for by the old lady, who took care of Lan's meals and also looked after the child.

Ms. Hoa also visited Lan many times to talk to, help, and comfort Lan.

Ms. Hoa also brought the necessary things for Lan's small child and some baby clothes.

Lan was moved to tears. She didn't expect that there would be such beautiful love in a foreign land.

Lan's family was still in her hometown, so Lan wrote back, sending pictures of the mother and child along with very emotional letters describing the situation of being petted by a new friend named Hoa, which prompted Lan's mother to tag along to respond to the letter with overwhelming gratitude.

After temporarily settling in Germany, Lan came up with the idea of inviting her mother on a trip to Germany. As a daughter, Lan always remembers her gentle mother. Lan believes her mother is the best mother in the world.

When Lan's child was two months old, Lan began to get healthier and she wanted to have the procedure done so that her child could live in Germany.

Therefore, Lan had to go to Czechoslovakia to do the necessary things to build a future for the child, and an innocent son was born.

One thing is that Lan is afraid to leave the temple because it would be too troublesome to leave her small child to the people in the temple. In addition, there will be a lot going on at the pagoda in the coming days as the number of people coming to Germany to apply for asylum increases. Therefore, the pagoda urgently needs helpers in many areas, especially food and water supplies.

There are many people doing the work, but it's not enough, so Lan keeps thinking about it.

At this time, Lan was thinking about returning to the Czech Republic, also known as Czechoslovakia, to ask her compatriots there to help her complete the necessary work because, Lan thought, the documents had to be official. To do this they would have to be legalized. Your child can live in peace and go to school normally in the future like other children growing up here.

A cold wind blew quickly through the place where three people were sitting and talking. Lan stopped talking and lazily stood up to greet Ly and Thuy. When Thuy saw this, he quickly said:

- If you need anything, we can try to help you. Just let me know how it all ends and we can sort things out, darling.

Lan responded emotionally in a choked voice:

- Yes.

Because Lan felt that there was no other way but to accept Thuy and Ly's help, even though they only knew each other, but in a foreign country, the love of compatriots is very valuable. With the help of Thuy and Ly, my child will be stable. Lan looked up at the sky, the sun was shining right in her face, she screamed:

- It's too hot, ladies.

Ly said to Thuy and Lan:

- Let's go then.

Then the three people left the store. Dark clouds formed small clusters into strange shapes that gradually flew into the distant sky. The wind blew gently through the long hair of three Asian women in Germany.

They walked hesitantly in the shadow of the sunset.

(...)

One afternoon, Ly was standing in the store selling goods after sending Lan back to Germany when she saw a group of men, looking decent in their foreign clothes, enter the store.

They communicated with each other in Vietnamese, so Ly understood what they needed. As she talked, Ly saw a man in the group keep looking at her. Ly heard them say to each other:

- Someone new has come here to do this.

Ly turned around and answered questions from other shoppers.

Nevertheless, these men also came up to her and tried to talk to her about it.

They wanted to buy products and after talking and asking questions, they found out that they came from Germany.

Among them is a man who is always quick and tries to get to Ly.

He called himself Quoc Viet, had lived in Germany for more than twenty years, was married and was about to get a divorce. He offered to invite Ly to dinner with him and the entire group from Germany.

In the days that followed, he kept coming to Ly and doing everything he could to get close to Ly.

He buys clothes for Ly. That evening he came to Ly:

- Your name is Ly, right?

His voice was loud and booming:

- Here I give you this beautiful bouquet of flowers.

He smiled humorously as he gave flowers:

- But you are also a flower, the petals are in chaos. ..Glass.

Ly accepted the bouquet of fresh flowers and burst out laughing. Wow, this is so much fun. Ly saw that the man named Quoc Viet in front of her looked like an actor. Viet saw Ly smile so he was no longer shy. He approached Ly, hugged her body tightly and said in a whisper:

No,

It's not like I said any pushy words

But actually, I already love you

Your heart is like an overflowing glass of water

How can I leave you now?

That day, after going out late at night, he invited Ly to his room at the hotel. He offered Ly wine to drink and said it was high quality French wine.

Ly still hesitated, then he pushed the glass of wine to Ly's lips and poured the wine into Ly's mouth.

Viet laughed loudly, satisfied with his work:

- It's great, it's great, you know how to enjoy the joys of life, right?

Ly wiped his mouth with his hand:

- Why do you keep forcing me to drink? I am not used to it.

Ly insisted on refusing. But the man still stubbornly refused to give up:

- Yes, you will gradually get used to it. Eating out with me without drinking wine is a waste. Let's have another glass to warm up, Ly.

My name is Ly, so I should raise my glass.

Doan Viet continued to pour wine for Ly.

In a dazed drunken state he began to sing jokingly:

Ly saw that the man's face was red and his voice was no longer continuous:

"And then I heard you singing

The singing voice is so peaceful

Baby, it's just because my heart is so weak

Makes me more and more restless »

Ly is happy to meet Viet, so she can't hold back. She allowed herself to surrender to the strong yeast of alcohol, as if she were drunk from a new love affair with a man much older than her.

The room was filled with bottles of wine and plates of food on the table. The loud, excited music on the television screen made Viet even more curious about the increased charm of Ly, the girl Viet had just met.

Afterwards, Ly got drunk and fell asleep in a small hotel room in the arms of a man who had a caterpillar-like beard on his lips...

...

When the man named Quoc Viet returned to Germany, he promised to take care of Ly and send money to the Czech side for Ly to consume in the coming days, especially when it is cold in winter. European activities were suspended for half a year. Quoc Viet told me before saying goodbye.

In the following days, Ly regularly received gifts and money from Quoc Viet, either by mail or via people from Germany to Czechoslovakia.

A few more months passed when Ly found out she was pregnant with Quoc Viet. While Ly was pregnant, Ly and Viet remained in regular contact for four months.

But after that Viet disappeared.

The letters sent from Germany with Ly's name on them were no longer there, which surprised even the postman. He said:

- Why doesn't Mr. Viet correspond with you anymore? You have a big belly.

Ly bit her lip and didn't answer. She thought casually:

- He's probably busy at work.

- How come I don't have time to write poems? Does he know you're pregnant?

- Have.

- That's so strange. Or call him. I have to ask her why, but she looks so pathetic.

- The line is not open, what should I do?

- Do you still have money to live on?

- It is enough to give birth two months later.

- Or you should go to Germany to find him.

- I want to go there too, but it's not that easy.

- If you plan to leave, I will find a way to help you.

After the postman left, Ly contacted Thao, a vendor at Sapa Market with whom Ly was very close. After exchanging stories for a long time, Thao realized that there was only one way for Ly to go to Germany to find the father of the fetus in Ly's womb.

Ly decided to go to Germany to find Viet with the fetus in his stomach.

When he traveled to Germany and arrived in the city, Viet gave him the address, but he could not find Viet anywhere and wandered around the train station for several days.

Ly was subsequently taken to a refugee camp by police so she could care for the fetus.

When asked why Ly came to Germany, Ly replied that she came here to find the father of her soon-to-be-born child.

Ly's statement did not result in Ly officially residing in Germany. But because she was pregnant and about to give birth, Ly temporarily stayed in the place where she knew the baby's father still lived.

One afternoon, when Ly went to the dry goods market at the Asia Store, she saw the boy named Hung who had gone to the Sapa market with Viet last year. She chased after him and asked him all the questions about Viet. He stammered:

- Don't ask me, I don't know!

But Ly didn't let him go and insisted on hearing Viet's news. Hung's face turned red and his breathing lost its rhythm due to temporary panic.

Ly saw Hang's stalking attitude and was also embarrassed. But only Hung can give Ly more information about Vietnam. That's why Ly has to hold on to Hung at all costs.

In the end, Hung fell in love and brought Ly De to Viet.

Viet was very confused when he met Ly again.

Meanwhile, Ly was impassive, looking at Viet without blinking. It seemed to her as if Viet hadn't changed at all in his body shape since the day they parted.

The man was strangely nervous, which confused Ly:

- Did you forget me? Your baby is about to be born.

- What, what are you saying, hey, calm down, why did you come here?

- Oh, you ask strangely, my baby is about to be born and you still act like a stranger to me?

- Let's take it slow, solve it slowly

Viet's treatment caused Ly to burst into tears and run away from Viet's house, in her ears as if she could hear the call of the man who had brought her indescribable joy and sadness. .

As the sun's shadow fell on the lawn in front of Quoc Viet's house, Ly was led into the house because Quoc Viet promised to make everything go smoothly for Ly.

In the days that followed, Ly's eyes became swollen. Ly cried a lot. She did not trust Quoc Viet with what he had promised. Ly finds it strange that Quoc Viet is so cold when they have a child together.

An indifferent mood that went so far that Ly couldn't understand whether Quoc Viet carried Ly's image in his heart or not.

Many nights Ly had nightmares, she saw a large hawk swooping down next to her and then flying away, her whole body shaking. Ly was afraid that she would feel like she was standing on the edge of a dark abyss, as dark as ink and as deep as if it had no bottom.

When I woke up, my whole body was shaking and covered in sweat. As Ly looked through the window bars, she saw the moon as if it were staring back at her.

Maybe the moon asked Ly if she needed help. As Ly looked at the first moon, she suddenly thought of her days in her hometown of Vietnam. Back then, Ly loved watching the moon, especially on full moon nights. On full moon nights, her mother says, her wishes come true when she prays. Her mother's words still resonate:

- If you pray in the moonlit nights, your prayers will be very effective, your prayers will soon be answered, my child.

- Oh, who will answer my prayers, mother?

Ly's mother replied gently:

- They are the higher ones, the heavens and the immortals, the fairies.

Thinking of this, Ly felt relieved, she smiled a little as she thought of her mother's gentle face.

So Ly lay down straight, folded his hands and closed his eyes. While she waited for her breathing to return to normal, Ly began to pray.

She asked for peace in her future life in the face of a life full of hardships and uncertainties in this foreign land.

After that, Ly had many conversations and heard her friends saying that such nightmares were just a common feeling of a pregnant woman, so Ly gradually became less worried. She lives only to take care of the child in her womb, waiting for the day to be born.

Thanks to Hung's help, Ly was able to go to the hospital to give birth in the following days when the day of labor came.

Fortunately, thanks to Hung's instructions and Hung's introduction to many other women with experience in pregnancy, Ly knows how to take care of her health and prevent complications. Pregnancy.

After giving birth, Ly was both tired and bored. She called home to tell her family the news, but then stopped and told them only briefly that she was still healthy.

Ly is very busy with her newborn baby, she constantly goes to the nurse to visit her baby and spends her free time only on things that are necessary for her life.

That day, after visiting her son, Ly went to the telephone room with the intention of calling her acquaintances. But the line is constantly busy. For a long time, Ly had little contact with family members, especially Ly's parents. Ly was also surprised, but because she was busy giving birth, she didn't have time to think about it. Today Ly also wanted to call back, but was busy on the other side.

Ly left the phone room and returned to her room, her mind empty.

Dreamily, Ly felt as if someone Ly was looking forward to calling was calling.

...

It seems like someone is looking at her and laughing at her, the giggle is so gentle that Ly turns around and rolls back and forth on the bed. She vaguely saw someone smiling at her. Who is that? Ly thought in the dream, but didn't say a word. She felt her entire body stiffen, as if she were being crushed by a shadow.

Then Ly heard the birds singing as if she was right outside her house in the past.

The sound of the door opening woke Lily up.

Ly opened his eyes and looked out. A person entering the room approaches Ly with open arms, in one hand she holds a bouquet of fresh flowers with petals, the name of which she knew when she was in the Czech Republic. It was the flower of the Time of Chaos... Ly.

At that moment, this empty heart made Ly forget everything in the world, only reality remained.

Seeing the petals as a sign of busy spring and extreme joy, Ly's soul swelled with emotion, and although her mouth smiled brightly, her eyes were full of tears. full of tears, tears of happiness, of the expected spring that is coming to her...

Then Ly heard a whisper in her ear, a familiar voice that Ly hadn't heard in a long time. She was gentle and gentle, but seemed to give Ly strength to live. Ly tried to calm down and opened his eyes to see who had just entered the room with such a familiar voice. Upon closer inspection with blurry eyes, it turned out to be an older woman with discolored but still healthy hair, who looked at Ly and smiled. A few seconds passed and Ly suddenly felt a lump in his throat. This feeling had to come from an invisible but deep, magical chain of emotions, if anything it came only from motherly love.

Ly murmured quietly:

- Mom, oh my God, it's my mom.

Through pale, teary eyes, Ly saw a very familiar face that she had missed for a long time.

The person whose long nights with the hardships of traveling and when she fell asleep, dimly hearing her mother's lullaby that she always carried in her heart, turned Ly into a machine, she automatically thought of that beautiful face.

Unexpectedly, Ly met her mother again today in a truly heartbreaking and bitter fateful situation. As always, from the beginning of humanity to today, mother's love is still the most sacred love. Ly howled in a stuttering voice, as if she were standing outside in the cold winter, her teeth chattering:

- Oh my God, why... are you... here?

Then Ly's tears flowed again, causing Ly's mother to look at her with concern:

- Hey, my child. Just take it slow and I'll tell you a story with a beginning, an end and a beginning.

Ly immediately sat up and got out of bed, although her health was unstable at the time. She was so happy that she was beside herself. Ly ran to get a chair to invite her mother to sit, and hurriedly ran to pour water, as if inviting a guest to visit her while she recovered from her illness.

- Mom, please tell me quickly so I can calm down. Why are you here? But where is my father, my mother?

When Ly left, police discovered that the mother's daughter had gone abroad to pay for the vacation. She screamed and told both mother and father to go to the police station to work. The invitation, which they called a subpoena, said they would work to send children abroad illegally and distribute assets abroad through reactionary intermediaries.

Ly's mother raised her hand to wipe away her tears.

- My father, he can't stand it. So he jumped up and argued with them. The police falsely accused your father of trying to attack someone on duty, my son...

- Oh dear God...

Ly cried out in surprise and hugged her thin mother, who was crying violently at the head of Ly's bed.

- Your father was temporarily detained at the police station, which is very far from our house.

Ly's mother sobbed as the afternoon sun faded, looking out the window at the many gray clouds drifting carelessly as if they didn't care about the pain of Ly and her gentle mother...

An ambulance with its green emergency lights on sped up to the hospital, its roaring noise drowning out the conversation between Ly and her mother. When Ly's mother saw this, she got up and said goodbye to Ly to leave. Ly held her mother's hand:

- Mom is going home, where are you going? Why don't you stay here with me?

- I have a temporary place to stay. Whenever I have free time, I will visit you again. Take care of your health. It has been such a long and miserable journey, my child. If I had known in advance that you would suffer like this, I would have preferred to let his brother go to do the work for you.

Ly also has an older brother who is still at home after Ly's departure.

When Ly heard her mother say this, she squeezed her mother's hand and whispered:

- Why are you saying that? Just let him do the business, mom.

Ly and her brother are very close, which is why Ly often says her brother's name, but rarely calls him by his usual name.

Hearing her say that, Ly suddenly thought of the conversation Ly's parents had before Ly went abroad with her aunt and uncle. Ly asked quietly:

- Is this what Uncle and Aunt Lan want, Mom?

- What are you asking to make it longer? Mom, let's go home now, it's already dark. "Mom still wants to check out the market here," she said, looking at Ly and smiling softly.

- But I want to know, mom, I don't want you to be pressured by others to do things.

Ly's mother sighed:

- That's terrible, no one forces or puts pressure on your parents, it's just how it is

In this situation there must be a way out, a solution that is good for the whole family.

That day my parents were very confused. My uncle and aunt Lan showed me a way to pass the exam. If they don't thank me, I won't, and what's wrong with me? Your aunt and uncle are very positive about this matter for your parents.

Then Ly's mother secretly looked at her daughter for a moment, looking silently through the glass wall in front of her, a motorcycle whizzed past her field of vision, then she breathed quietly, stood up and walked out the door. The sun had completely gone out, so the room was dark. Ly was still kneeling on the bed, thinking endlessly...

The next day, Ly heard her mother telling the whole story about Ly's death and no one else's.

At that time, Ly's brother had just signed a contract to carry out cultural and artistic work in preparation for a program called "Foreign Festival", so the young man resolutely refused to listen to his parents and uncle. Aunt Lan should go.

--

According to her mother, Ly's brother screamed during the conversation, including Aunt Lan:

- Wow, the work ahead of me is so chaotic, I'm doing so well, but my aunt and uncle, my parents told me to give up everything and go abroad indefinitely. Also, I was only promised a joint business contract, I can't break a promise with anyone.

Mom asked again:

- Is your new job so secure that you trust them? Again, just like before. Times of wisdom are difficult, my love, think carefully.

The aunt begged him:

- I went abroad and tried to learn more there.

Ly's brother's mother also added a lot, but he insisted that he had already signed the cooperation agreement.

Ly's mother told Ly that at that time she was extremely saddened by the disrespectful attitude of her son, who, although he had grown up, had grown up and had a large body, but in her opinion was still naive and unable to adapt to life's circumstances in a timely manner . This can also be an indication that the parents were unable to raise their children at the time. Life is inherently a struggle coupled with social insecurities.

She said Ly's brother even tried to argue:

- Besides, I was just promised a business contract, I can't break my promise to anyone.

Mom asked again:

- Is your new job safe if you trust them? Just like before, it's just more suffering. These are difficult times, my child, think carefully.

Ly's mother continued:

- Your uncle and aunt Lan also had to speak but couldn't convince their brother.

The aunt begged him:

- I'm going abroad and trying to learn more there.

Ly's brother's mother also added a lot, but he insisted on the excuse that he had already signed the cooperation agreement.

So Ly's brother decided not to go abroad, no matter how much his parents, aunts and uncles explained to him.

After all, no one wanted the solution of letting Ly go abroad alone.

But if there is no one else in the house, you have to accept it.

Aunt Lan thought for a few days before contacting Ly's mother.

The aunt hesitated when she made the suggestion:

- Or like this: It's okay to let Ly go abroad.

In the end, Ly became the solution to save the family.

The sky went completely dark when Ly's mother stopped talking to take a drink of water. Ly felt sorry for her mother, so she sniffed and almost cried loudly.

Shoulders tremble. Ly's mother continued, her voice as calm as the sound of rain falling outside the hospital:

- Even my brother...

She smacked her mouth and sighed deeply.

Ly stood up:

- How is he, mother?

Ly's mother continued:

- He also has problems at his film job.

The rain suddenly stopped, the room became brighter, Ly's mother stopped talking and created a quiet space in the room.

- His contract was terminated at the film company, so no part of him could be seen in the film.

- It's so miserable, how is it supposed to work, mom?

- It's crazy, baby.

It must have been weeks since he couldn't eat or sleep. Your father is very scared and your mother feels like she's on fire.

From that day on, my mother was afraid to ask him anything, but only silently prayed that he would continue to have another job.

-   Luckily...
- What do you mean by luck, mom? She took another sip of water, a light breeze blew through the hair on her forehead, Ly looked at her mother sympathetically. Ly thought about the time when she was at home when her mother took good care of her hair and washed it with a fragrant scent. Ly's mother also often combs her hair long to make it straight. She often said that hair is very important for a girl to enhance her charm.

But now she ignores everything to take care of her beloved children.

Suddenly she remembered the time when she took the train alone from her house to Hai-Phong Port and from there had to take a ship abroad. The journey lasted almost two months and was full of hardships that she could endure.

She thinks about the days when she got seasick at sea and had to be taken to a private room for treatment because her stomach wouldn't do what she wanted. It also took a week before she could eat and drink normally again.

She was very touched by the nurse on the train who was worried about her.

This time she was seasick, so she was unstable and fell.

If the nurse hadn't helped her in time, she would have fallen and hit her head on the hard iron wall of the train. If something like that happened, she would probably regret it for the rest of her life.

When the nurse was able to take her body, she no longer had a soul. At that moment she screamed loudly:

- Oh, is this Ly, please help me into the room. Mom died so quickly. I'm so dizzy.

She spoke as if she were at home, as if her beloved daughter Ly had always been with her since she was a child.

- No, it's me, grandma. My name is Tam, the nurse on the ship.

Then she was frightened and said awkwardly to the nurse named Tam:

- Thank you, please give me seasickness tablets. I want to vomit so badly, since morning until now.

- Yes, Tam will bring it to you immediately. He went to his room to rest and relieve the fatigue.

Then Nurse Tam brought her the medicine and carefully explained how to use it. She told her:

- Uncle, old people often suffer from this. Tam's parents used to get seasick on boat trips. I need to lie down and rest to feel less tired.

Thanks to nurse Tam, she felt less lonely in the following days and often spent the days of her wonderful journey talking.

Ly's mother scribbled in silence and said to herself:

- If you change your mind, you must obey the law.

If you encounter difficulties, you must accept the agreement and deal with it appropriately in the interest of peace between the parties. Even Ly's aunt and uncle Lan had to accept the trip to complete the household chores smoothly.

Then she continued in a monotone voice:

- Luckily he shared a script or story, so he jumped to another place to continue after revising the script a bit.

- I heard that social stories about chaos should be popular.

Actually, it is thanks to this father and son that he advises this.

If not, woe to him, just because people have so much power that they can't do it.

I have to thoughtfully mention my husband and children again

Here she suddenly sighed. Because of her husband is also difficult and stubborn. He refused to let his son defeat him, but then had to give in and give something to his son. People still say that raising children until 99 still has to take care of everything and that's just because of the tears. My grandparents told me.

Then she turned to comfort her daughter:

- Come on, we must live in faith and hope, my child. Everyone knows that life will never be the way we want it to be, so we have to strive, we have to try for tomorrow, because after winter there will be a bright spring.

When Ly heard her mother's words, she was surprised. Why was her mother so literary today?

This thought suddenly made Ly laugh and also made Ly's mother laugh.

Ly said to her mother:

- I really like spring, mom. Because of in spring many beautiful flowers bloom in all colors.

- But... Spring is already here, mom?

Ly's mother laughed loudly and looked at her daughter with emotion on her wrinkled face.

- It would be great if my father and brother were here now.

Thinking about her husband and children made Ly's mother uncomfortable.

Then she thought about her husband's family, thought about Mr. and Mrs. Lan, who Ly's aunt and uncle, and wondered if her calculations would go smoothly and go as planned? When she thought about the turmoil in her life, she felt sad. Everyone is like that. Who doesn't want to have a good plan for their life, their family and their children? But there is also God. The success of any plan is determined by the green man, that is, by the sky. Therefore, she believed that the verses in the famous "Kieu Story" by the great Vietnamese poet Nguyen-Du made the situation of her mother and daughter clear expressed:

"All things are brought about by God.

Man was born with a body by God. Therefore he has a good or bad life only according to the will of God."

She felt very comforted by this thought. When we are in the cycle of creation, we must accept that we have only created karma for ourselves. Ly's mother constantly reflected on the verses of poet Nguyen Cong Tru, a poet with a politics of leisure enjoyment that her husband often mentioned , as if to remind them to find an acceptance of ups and downs through the flow of human life. Her husband told her that as the couple drank tea and chatted together one autumn evening:

- Only when we happily accept reality can we exist without being wasted.

Then he read Nguyen Cong Tru's poem to   her:
"Please don't be human in your next life." Be a pine tree standing in the middle of the sky and ringing.

In the middle of the sky there are steep cliffs. He who can endure the cold will Climbing with the jaws»These verses are repeated again and again by her husband, so that she can still remember them very well.

Then he advised her with a loving look, her husband's eyes lit up as if he was giving her strength in life:

-Let's be like a pine tree that, despite all odds, still stands tall in the middle of the sky, grandma.

As she thought about her husband's words back then, she was simultaneously worried about him and secretly accused him of making mistakes in life just out of ambition.

To say that personal ambition is not entirely true, but it also includes things that concern the whole family with her and her children.

Maybe it was the things that pushed the family, but also a punishment for the mistakes in his life, for which she was also partially responsible.

She thought about her youth, when the two of them were newly married.

He promised her a lot back then, especially concern for the family's happiness, because it is a home for both of them, a happiness without limits.

Therefore, both of them try to make sacrifices for each other and sometimes forget about the privacy of their unmarried life.

But as the years passed, so did the details of the couple's life.

Her husband began to pursue separate directions in life.

At times he was seen sitting meditating for hours, and then he was constantly distracted by housework.

She started to get upset. But then the suffering made her silently accept it and the sadness also grew day by day.

But now she was standing in front of her beloved daughter, from whom she had been separated for so long.

That's why she feels obliged to create a responsibility warm and loving atmosphere of holy motherly love.

- Turning to her daughter, she felt that she had to give her joy after many difficult and hard days.

It's about leaving, about a personal love and so on and so forth.

Just like the picture of her beloved husband, who has recently been following closely in her footsteps.

She looked at Ly with eyes filled with the eternal love between mother and child.

Then mother and daughter hugged in the dark, but it was just a curtain

The night of spring returns to a life full of hope for a bright tomorrow.

Trường Hà Vũ Toại *(Vũ Duy Toại)*

136   Has spring already arrived

Author's pseudonym:

The author's real name is Vũ Duy Toại.

The existing pseudonym is Trường Hà.

The author published literary and art books, poetry collections, music collections and short story collections under this name

Trường Hà Vũ Toại

Has spring already arrived

Already published:

Poetry (collection of poems) by the same author:

The love that still remains within me

Publishing year:

2020 in Vietnamese - 2023 in German

Music collection (book) 1, 2, 3, 4, 5

directed by the author in Vietnamese.

Years of publication: 2020, 2021, 2022, 2023.

Has spring already arrived

Year of publication: 2020 in Vietnamese

The reconstruction of life

Year of publication: 2019 in Vietnamese